GOODNIGHT, GRIZZLE GRUMP!

By Aaron Blecha

HARPER
An Imprint of HarperCollinsPublishers

Goodnight, Grizzle Grump!

For information address HarperCollins Children's Books, a division of HarperCollins Publishers, 195 Broadway, New York, NY 10007.
www.harpercollinschildrens.com

ISBN 978-0-06-229746-4

The artist used Prismacolor Col-Erase Carmine Red and Blue pencils on Strathmore Bristol Vellum and Photoshop to create the illustrations for this book.
Typography by Rachel Zegar. Hand lettering by Aaron Blecha.
15 16 17 18 19 SCP 10 9 8 7 6 5 4 3 2 1
❖
First Edition

For Betsy & Olive—
my two greatest
creations

Deep in the dark forest, where no man has ever set foot, lives a creature quite grouchy who goes by the name of . . .

GRIZZLE
GRUMP!

Autumn is here and it's time for Grizzle Grump to hibernate.

So with a polite

Grizzle Grump shuffles off in search of a quiet place to sleep.

After finding the perfect spot in the trees . . .

Grizzle Grump

SCRATCHES

and he

SNIFFS,

then he

TEETERS

and he

TOTTERS.

Next he

WIGGLES

and he

WOBBLES,

he FLIPS

and FLOPS!

Finally he SNOOZES and SNORES. . . .

"What's all that NOISE?!?"
NIK NOK NIK NOK
NIK NOK
NIK NOK
NIK NOK
NIK NOK

With a
grumble!

And a
mumble!

Grizzle Grump lumbers off in
search of a quieter place to sleep.

AHA!

"This stream looks like a peaceful place for a long winter snooze!"

After finding the perfect spot next to the brook . . .

Grizzle Grump

SCRATCHES

and he

SNIFFS,

then he

TEETERS

and he

TOTTERS.

Next he

WIGGLES

and he

WOBBLES,

he

FLIPS

and

FLOPS!

Finally he

SNOOZES

and

SNORES. . . .

"What's all that NOISE?!?"
WHAP
WHUMP
WHAP
WHUMP
WHAP
WHUMP
WHAP
WHUMP
WHAP
WHUMP
WHAP
WHUMP

Grizzle Grump stumbles off in search of a quieter place to sleep.

"I'm sure to sleep like a log
in this dark, gloomy swamp!"

After finding the perfect spot in the marsh . . .

Grizzle Grump

SCRATCHES

and he

SNIFFS,

then he

TEETERS

and he

TOTTERS.

Next he

WIGGLES

and he

WOBBLES,

he FLIPS

and FLOPS!

Finally he

SNOOZES

and

SNORES. . . .

"What's all that NOISE?!?"
EEERP MEERP
EEERP MEERP
EEERP MEERP
EEERP MEERP

With a
huff!

And a
puff!

Grizzle Grump stomps off in search of a quieter place to sleep.

"Surely there's somewhere here on this high mountaintop where I can take my long winter nap!"

Tired out and trembling,
Grizzle Grump stumbles in.

But there's
no scratching,
no sniffing.

No teetering,
no tottering.

No wiggling,
no wobbling.

And definitely
no flipping!
Just a great
big flopping!
!?!
FLOP!

"It's time for
ME TO HIBERNATE!"

SLAM!
Until Spring!

Finally Grizzle Grump falls into a deep sleep. His loud snores echo out of the cave and throughout the woods.

SHUSH!
EEERP MEERP
INSIDE VOICES!
HOOP HOLLA!
ZIP IT!
CHIRP MIRP!
TURN IT DOWN!
NIK NOK
HUSH!
HERM LERM!
WE GOTTA GET OUT OF HERE!
BURP BELLOW!
LET'SSSS GO!
HISS FISS!

"Sweet dreams,
Grizzle Grump!"